USBORNE HOTSHOTS

HISTORY OF BRITAIN

USBORNE HOTSHOTS
HISTORY
OF BRITAIN

Lisa Miles and Anne Millard
Designed by Fiona Johnson

Series editor: Judy Tatchell
Series designer: Ruth Russell

CONTENTS

Note on dates

The year 0 is taken as the year of Christ's birth. BC means "before Christ". AD (*anno domini* – Latin for "the year of the Lord") means after his birth. Dates for which no letters are given are AD.

When dates appear with a "c." before them, this means that the date is not certain. The "c." stands for *circa*, which is Latin for "about".

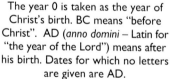
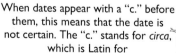

Early Britain

c.4000BC Farming comes to Britain

An early farm

Around 4000BC, farming people from mainland Europe arrived in Britain. Before this, people in Britain had been nomads, hunting animals and gathering plants for food. By 3500BC, farming had taken over from this hunting and gathering lifestyle and people began to settle in permanent shelters.

c.2000BC Stonehenge

In early times great circles of stone or wood, called henges, were built. No one knows what they were for, but they may have been used for sacred ceremonies to do with sun worship. The most famous henge in Britain is Stonehenge.

Stonehenge, near Salisbury. It was built between 2300 and 1540BC.

55BC The Romans invade

In 55BC, Britain was invaded by the Romans, led by Julius Caesar. The Romans came from central Italy and conquered a huge empire. In 54BC, Caesar forced the British to agree to pay money, called a

EUROPE
Roman Empire in AD100

tribute, to Rome. In AD43, the Romans invaded again and this time occupied Britain. They set up their own administrative and legal systems, built roads, created new towns and even introduced the alphabet we use today.

AD61 Boudicca's rebellion

Boudicca was queen of a British tribe called the Iceni. In AD61, she led the Britons in an uprising against their Roman conquerors. She was eventually defeated and committed suicide.

A typical Roman-built British town

AD122 Hadrian's Wall

Hadrian's Wall

Over the next 50 years, the Romans extended their control over England and Wales. Much of Scotland (then known as Caledonia) remained unconquered. The Romans never tried to conquer Ireland.

Tribes from Scotland, called the Picts, often raided England. In AD122, the Roman Emperor Hadrian ordered a wall to be built as a frontier to keep the Picts out. Parts of it are still there today.

c.AD304 The death of St. Alban

The Romans introduced Christianity to Britain in the 3rd century. At times, however, it was banned during the Roman Empire. In AD304, St. Alban became the first British martyr (a person who dies for a belief) when he was beheaded for being a Christian. St. Patrick later carried Christianity from Britian to Ireland in the 5th century.

c.AD435 The Anglo-Saxons arrive

In the 5th century, the Roman Empire grew weak and began to break up. Tribes from mainland Europe, called Angles, Saxons and Jutes, took advantage of this and invaded Britain.

The decorated helmet of an Anglo-Saxon king

These Anglo-Saxons occupied most of England. Some native Britons fled to Wales, Cornwall and Britanny (in France) to escape them. Others submitted to the invaders. By the 7th century, England (which received its name from the word Angle) was made up of seven Anglo-Saxon kingdoms.

The seven Anglo-Saxon kingdoms

SCOTLAND

Northumbria

WALES

Mercia
ENGLAND

East Anglia

Essex

Kent

Wessex

CORNWALL

Sussex

AD597 St. Augustine's mission

The Anglo-Saxons were pagans – they believed in their own gods, not the Christian God. In AD597, Pope Gregory I sent a man called Augustine with forty monks to convert them. The Anglo-Saxon King Aethelbert of Kent allowed the monks to settle in Canterbury and was later baptized a Christian by Augustine. For this, the Church recognized Augustine as a saint.

AD782 Offa's Dyke

Mercia became the dominant kingdom in England under King Offa, who ruled from 757 to 796. He was the first English king to make coins.

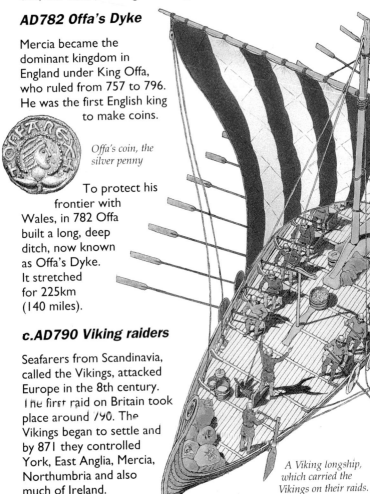

Offa's coin, the silver penny

To protect his frontier with Wales, in 782 Offa built a long, deep ditch, now known as Offa's Dyke. It stretched for 225km (140 miles).

c.AD790 Viking raiders

Seafarers from Scandinavia, called the Vikings, attacked Europe in the 8th century. The first raid on Britain took place around 790. The Vikings began to settle and by 871 they controlled York, East Anglia, Mercia, Northumbria and also much of Ireland.

A Viking longship, which carried the Vikings on their raids.

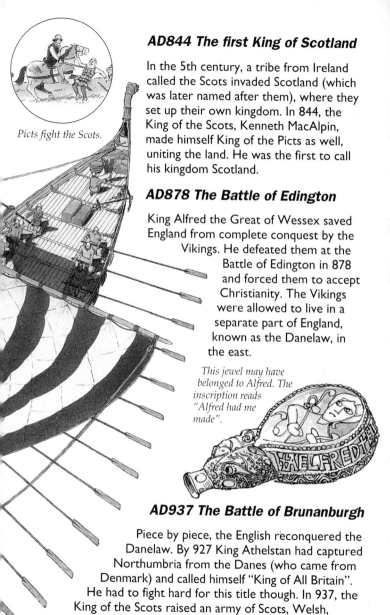

AD844 The first King of Scotland

In the 5th century, a tribe from Ireland called the Scots invaded Scotland (which was later named after them), where they set up their own kingdom. In 844, the King of the Scots, Kenneth MacAlpin, made himself King of the Picts as well, uniting the land. He was the first to call his kingdom Scotland.

Picts fight the Scots.

AD878 The Battle of Edington

King Alfred the Great of Wessex saved England from complete conquest by the Vikings. He defeated them at the Battle of Edington in 878 and forced them to accept Christianity. The Vikings were allowed to live in a separate part of England, known as the Danelaw, in the east.

This jewel may have belonged to Alfred. The inscription reads "Alfred had me made".

AD937 The Battle of Brunanburgh

Piece by piece, the English reconquered the Danelaw. By 927 King Athelstan had captured Northumbria from the Danes (who came from Denmark) and called himself "King of All Britain". He had to fight hard for this title though. In 937, the King of the Scots raised an army of Scots, Welsh, Britons and Danes against him. They met at the Battle of Brunanburgh in Scotland, where Athelstan triumphed.

The Middle Ages

This strip of tapestry...

...called the Bayeux Tapestry...

...shows the Norman invasion...

...and King Harold's death.

1066 The Norman Conquest

William, Duke of Normandy, had been promised the English throne. When Edward the Confessor died, the throne was given to Harold of Wessex instead. To win his throne, William invaded and defeated Harold at the Battle of Hastings in 1066. William "the Conqueror" took control of England. The Normans also spread into Wales, southern Scotland and Ireland but failed to conquer them.

1163 The first university

In 1163 the first university in Britain was founded at Oxford to educate men who were to become priests. It attracted many pupils and became one of the most important universities in Europe. Cambridge University was founded later in 1274.

1170 Death of Thomas à Becket

King Henry II of England made his friend Thomas à Becket Archbishop of Canterbury, in order to gain influence over the Church. Becket, however, put the Church's interests before Henry's. This angered him and in a rage he is said to have wished to be rid of Becket. Four knights rode to Canterbury and murdered Becket in the cathedral, shocking the Christian world.

King...

...versus Church.

1171 Henry becomes Irish overlord

In 1171, Henry II landed in Ireland after becoming involved in a dispute between two Irish kings. Henry became overlord of the Irish and this was the first time that Ireland had been under English rule.

1189 Crusade!

In 1096, many European Christians set off to Syria and Palestine to fight the Muslims, then known as Saracens, who had captured Jerusalem – holy city of Jews, Muslims and Christians. These wars against the Saracens are called the Crusades. King Richard I of England, the Lionheart, set off on the Third Crusade in 1189. He won victories over the Saracens, but never captured Jerusalem.

A Christian Crusader fights a Saracen.

1215 The Magna Carta

After Richard died, his brother John came to the throne, but he argued with the barons, his noblemen. Finally in 1215, they forced him to sign an agreement, called the Magna

Carta, at Runnymede. This stated, among other things, that the king had to consult the barons over important issues, such as taxation.

1282 The last Welsh Prince

In 1254 Llewellyn ap Gruffydd became sole Welsh ruler. Henry III recognized him as Prince of Wales and in return Llewellyn accepted Henry as his overlord, but fighting still went on between the Welsh and the English. When Llewellyn was killed in 1282, the title Prince of Wales was taken by the eldest son of the English King Edward I.

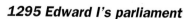

The Welsh flag

1295 Edward I's parliament

In 1295, Edward I set up the first true parliament in England. Each town and shire (county) sent two spokesmen to represent them. Barons, bishops and abbots were also present.

Edward's parliament

1314 The Battle of Bannockburn

Robert Bruce

The English kings were overlords of the Scots, but the Scots rebelled and in 1306, Robert Bruce assumed leadership and was crowned at Scone. He defeated the English in 1314 at Bannockburn and Scotland was recognized as an independent country in 1328.

1337 The Hundred Years' War begins

In 1337 a war broke out between England and France which was to last, on and off, for over a hundred years. It began when Edward III laid claim to the French throne. The English gained control of much of France, but when the wars ended in 1453, the only territory in France left to the English was Calais.

1348 The Black Death

In 1347, a terrible outbreak of the Black Death (bubonic plague) came to Europe. It was carried by fleas living on black rats. A third of the entire population died within 18 months. It spread like wildfire, reaching England in 1348.

To stop the plague spreading, clothes belonging to its victims were burned.

c.1377 Wycliffe's Bible

John Wycliffe was a religious reformer, who believed that everyone should be able to understand the Bible, which was traditionally written in Latin. He translated it into English, infuriating Church leaders.

1381 The Peasants' Revolt

In 1381, the government passed a poll-tax (a tax on every person) to pay for war against the French. The peasants were already discontented and a revolt broke out led by Wat Tyler from Kent. He gathered a peasant army and marched on London. Richard II granted them their demands, but Tyler was stabbed to death the next day and Richard's promises were all broken.

A peasant farm worker

1455 The Wars of the Roses

In 1455, a war broke out between two families – Lancaster and York. Both sides were descendents of Edward III and each believed that they had a better right to the throne. For over 40 years, kings from both sides were crowned and deposed.

The red rose of Lancaster

The white rose of York

1476 Caxton's press

In 1476 William Caxton set up the first printing press in Britain, at Westminster. He went on to print 96 books including Chaucer's *Canterbury Tales*, written in 1383. One of the most famous works in English, it tells the tales told by a group of pilgrims on a journey.

1483 The Princes in the Tower

In 1483, Edward V came to the throne, aged 13. After two months, Edward and his brother Richard were imprisoned by their uncle in the Tower of London. The boys disappeared and their uncle seized the throne as Richard III. Most people think that the boys were murdered, but disagree about who did it. Richard was later killed at the Battle of Bosworth in 1485, when Henry VII became the first Tudor King.

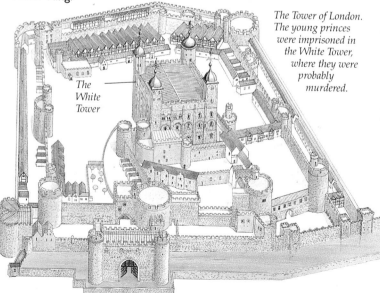

The Tower of London. The young princes were imprisoned in the White Tower, where they were probably murdered.

The White Tower

Tudors and Stuarts

1533 Henry VIII's divorce

Henry VIII was the second king in the great Tudor dynasty. He is best remembered for having six wives – Catherine of Aragon, Anne Boleyn, Jane Seymour, Anne of Cleves, Katherine Howard and Catherine Parr. He divorced his first wife in 1533 because he had no male heir. To do this, Henry had to break with the Catholic Church, which had governed Christianity in England since 664.

1536 The Church of England

In 1536, Henry made himself Head of the Church of England. The Church was very rich and Henry took many of its riches for himself by closing down convents and monasteries. Between 1536 and 1539, most were sold or destroyed in the Dissolution of the Monasteries.

1536 The first Poor Law

Also in 1536, in an attempt to deal with unemployment, Henry VIII passed the first Poor Law. This law instructed each parish to be responsible for looking after its own poor people.

1553 The nine days' queen

The boy king, Edward VI, was persuaded by the Duke of Northumberland to name as his heir his cousin instead of his sister Mary. His cousin, Lady Jane Grey, was married to Northumberland's son. When Edward died in 1553, Jane ruled for only nine days before Mary seized power. Jane, her husband and both their fathers were all executed.

Henry VIII was a popular monarch. He ruled from 1509-1547.

12

1554 Bloody Mary marries Philip of Spain

Mary Tudor was Catholic, but the Church of England had become Protestant after Henry VIII's break with Catholicism. Mary now reinstated Catholicism and many who refused to convert were executed. For this reason, she became known as Bloody Mary. In 1554, she married Philip II of Spain. This made her even more unpopular as England and Spain were rivals.

1558 Elizabeth I comes to the throne

Mary Tudor died childless and her sister Elizabeth succeeded her in 1558. Elizabeth I ruled England during a golden age of trade, exploration and power. She reigned for 45 years. During her reign, she took steps to halt rising prices and unemployment by recalling the old coinage and issuing new money. She also reinstated Henry VIII's laws regarding the Church and became Head of the Church of England herself. In 1563 its principles were defined in the Thirty Nine Articles.

Elizabeth I

1580 Drake sails around the world

In 1580, Francis Drake completed his voyage around the world. This brave journey had taken two years and ten months and Drake was the first Englishman to achieve it.

Elizabeth I later boarded Drake's ship and knighted him for his achievement.

1587 Mary Queen of Scots is executed

In 1559 Elizabeth's cousin, the Catholic Mary Queen of Scots, laid claim to the English throne. Many Catholics wanted her as queen and she became involved in several plots against Elizabeth. She was finally executed in Fotheringhay Castle in 1587.

Mary Queen of Scots

1588 The Spanish Armada

England and Spain were great rivals. Their ships attacked each other off America, where Spain had extensive colonies. Philip II of Spain gathered together a fleet, called the Armada, with which to invade England. In 1588 it set sail, but the English set fire to many of its ships and the rest were destroyed by storms.

The Spanish Armada

1598 The Globe Theatre

Drama, arts and music flourished during the Elizabethan age and in 1598, work began on the Globe Theatre in London. During the reigns of Elizabeth I and James I, the Globe saw the production of the plays of William Shakespeare, the great poet and playwright.

1603 James I

In 1603, James VI of Scotland became James I of England, the first Stuart king. The crowns of Scotland and England were now united. James believed in the Divine Right of Kings – the belief that monarchs are responsible only to God. He tried to rule without Parliament for long periods, which made him unpopular.

The Globe Theatre in London – a typical playhouse.

James I, son of Mary Queen of Scots.

14

1605 The Gunpowder Plot

Guy Fawkes

James I was a strict Protestant and soon after he came to the throne, a group of Catholics laid a plot to kill him. Their plan was to blow up the King and his ministers in Parliament on November 5, 1605. The plot was betrayed and one of the gang, Guy Fawkes, was caught with gunpowder in the cellars. He and the others were later executed.

1620 The Pilgrim Fathers

In 1620 a group of Puritans (extreme Protestants), who disliked England's religious laws, emigrated to North America in a ship called the *Mayflower*. They set up a successful colony at New Plymouth, Massachusetts. During the seventeenth century, the British founded 13 colonies along the east coast of North America.

The Pilgrims

1642 The Civil War in England

Charles I, like his father James I, often argued with Parliament. In 1642, civil war broke out in England. On one side were the Royalists who supported Charles, and on the other were the Parliamentarians, supported by the Scots. This bitter war lasted six years. In 1648 the Scots changed sides and declared war in support of Charles. Charles, however, was eventually captured and the Royalists were defeated.

A Parliamentarian stabs a Royalist.

1649 Charles I is executed

Charles I was put on trial for treason (betrayal of his country) and was found guilty. He was beheaded in Whitehall in 1649 and for the first time since the Saxon age, Britain was without a king or queen.

1649 The Commonwealth

Oliver Cromwell

In 1649 a republic (a country where the head of state is not a king or queen) was set up. Known as the Commonwealth, its ruler was Oliver Cromwell, leader of the Parliamentarians. Like King Charles before him, Cromwell could not get on with Parliament and in 1653 he dismissed it and became Lord Protector.

1660 Restoration of the Monarchy

After Cromwell's death, Parliament invited Charles I's son to return from France and become King Charles II. The monarchy (rule of a king or queen) was restored in 1660.

Charles II

1666 Fire follows plague

In 1665, Britain was devastated by the plague – an attack of the Black Death. In London alone 68,000 people died. The situation was desperate. Then in 1666 a huge fire, known as the Great Fire of London, raged through the capital for four days. The fire helped to rid the city of plague by killing the rats which spread the disease.

The Great Fire started in a baker's shop in Pudding Lane. It destroyed four-fifths of the city, burning down all the old wooden buildings of the Middle Ages.

1673 St. Paul's Cathedral

St. Paul's

After the Great Fire, the architect Christopher Wren presented plans to rebuild London. His plans were rejected, but some years later he resubmitted plans for St. Paul's which were approved. Work began in 1673 and was completed in 1711.

1689 The Glorious Revolution

James II was a Catholic and during his reign he upset most of his Protestant subjects. James had a son which meant that another Catholic would reign after him. James's daughter Mary was married to the Protestant Prince William of Orange in the Netherlands. Parliament asked them to take the throne, so they invaded and James fled. The return of Protestants to the throne is known as the Glorious Revolution.

1689 The Battle of the Boyne

In the seventeenth century, conflicts arose in Ireland between Catholics and Protestants. In 1689, the exiled James II landed an army in Ireland and was welcomed by many Irish. However, he was defeated by William of Orange, who was fighting for his throne, at the Battle of the Boyne. From then on, Protestants were known as Orangemen.

William of Orange

1704 The Battle of Blenheim

In 1701, Britain became involved in the War of the Spanish Succession. It joined forces with Austria and the Netherlands to prevent Louis XIV of France's grandson becoming King of Spain. The Duke of Marlborough commanded the British and won great victories, including the Battle of Blenheim in 1704. In return for his service to the nation, Blenheim Palace in Oxfordshire was built for him.

Blenheim Palace

The eighteenth century

c.1700 The Agricultural Revolution begins

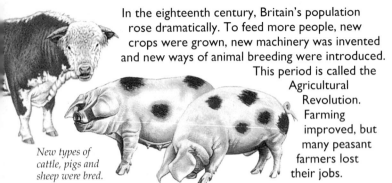

In the eighteenth century, Britain's population rose dramatically. To feed more people, new crops were grown, new machinery was invented and new ways of animal breeding were introduced. This period is called the Agricultural Revolution. Farming improved, but many peasant farmers lost their jobs.

New types of cattle, pigs and sheep were bred.

1714 The Hanoverian dynasty begins

In 1714, the throne passed to the Elector of Hanover in Germany, who became King George I. He spoke no English and left decisions to his ministers. From this time, the importance of Parliament grew.

Scottish Members of Parliament (MPs) had voted for union with England in 1707 and now sat in the Houses of Parliament in London. Scotland kept its own legal system and its own Presbyterian Church.

The British Parliament in the early 18th century

1720 The South Sea Bubble

In 1719, the South Sea Company (which had been set up to trade in the Pacific) took over the National Debt – money owed by the government to the Bank of England. People were given shares in the South Sea Company instead of money they were owed. At first they were worth a lot, but in 1720 the price fell and investors lost heavily. Many politicians had sold their shares quickly beforehand, which led to a scandal known as the South Sea Bubble.

A £20 banknote from 1759

1732 The first Prime Minister

George I's chief minister was Robert Walpole, who ran the government on the King's behalf. In 1732, his fellow MPs began to call him the "Prime Minister". This title, however, was not used officially until 1905.

Robert Walpole

1745 Bonnie Prince Charlie

In 1745, an attempt was made to put James II's grandson, Bonnie Prince Charlie, on the throne. The Prince's followers, called the Jacobites, won the Battle of Prestonpans in Scotland and marched into England as far as Derby. Most English people, however, did not want to put a Catholic king back on the throne. The Jacobites retreated and were defeated at the Battle of Culloden in 1746.

Bonnie Prince Charlie

c.1750 The Industrial Revolution

From the 1750s, new inventions and the discovery of steam as a power source led to the improvement of industry. Factories were set up and manufacturers produced more goods, quicker and more cheaply. Towns grew up around the factories and many people moved there to find work. In the towns, however, conditions were dirty, cramped and unhealthy.

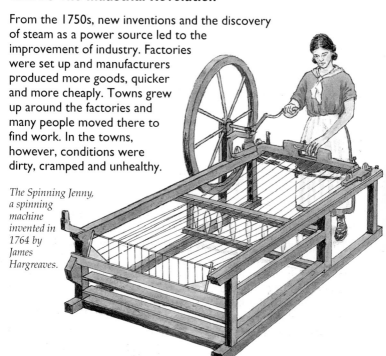

The Spinning Jenny, a spinning machine invented in 1764 by James Hargreaves.

1757 Clive of India

Clive meeting the Nawab of Bengal after the Battle of Plassey.

In the eighteenth century, Britain was represented in India by the East India Trading Company, which was also responsible for governing the areas under British rule. (Trading and governing were separated in 1858.) In 1757 Robert Clive, known as Clive of India, led the British to victory over Bengal in the Battle of Plassey. The British were now masters of all the east coast of India.

1759 The Battle of Quebec

During the eighteenth century, Britain and France took part in a power struggle for control of North America. In 1759, the British won control of Canada at the Battle of Quebec, led by General James Wolfe. In 1761, Canada became a British colony.

British territory after 1763

1768 Cook's first voyage

As Britain gained territory in North America and Asia, Captain James Cook set out in 1768 on the first of his three great voyages to explore the Pacific Ocean. Cook explored the coasts of both Australia and New Zealand and claimed them for Britain. He landed in Australia, at a spot which he named Botany Bay. Australia was first used as a colony for convicts, but settlers soon outnumbered them.

Cook's chronometer – an aid to navigation

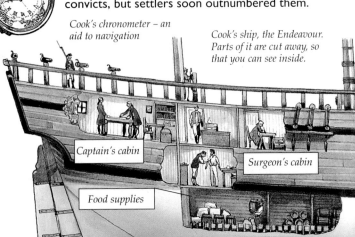

Cook's ship, the Endeavour. Parts of it are cut away, so that you can see inside.

Captain's cabin

Surgeon's cabin

Food supplies

1769 Wedgwood's factory

In 1769, Josiah Wedgwood opened a pottery factory at Etruria near Stoke-on-Trent. He recognized the importance of canals and invested in them so that he could transport his fragile goods more safely and cheaply.

1775 The American War of Independence

In the second half of the eighteenth century, some European colonists in North America began to resent British control over them. They especially resented having to pay taxes to Britain, while they had no say in the British Parliament. In 1775, this led to the American War of Independence. The colonists, led by George Washington, defeated the British. The colonies were renamed the United States of America.

American colonists pulling down a statue of George III.

1779 The first iron bridge

In 1779 the first ever iron bridge in the world was built near Coalbrookdale, Shropshire, England. Better methods of iron production in the Industrial Revolution led to this achievement.

1782 Watt's steam engine

In 1782, the Scottish engineer James Watt invented the rotary steam engine, an improvement on earlier steam engines because it could drive other machines. Steam power became the main source of power in the textile mills. The engine also made possible the invention of the steam train in the early nineteenth century.

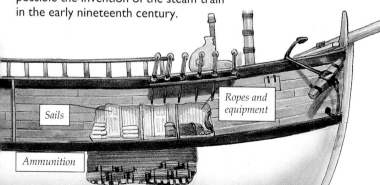

Sails

Ropes and equipment

Ammunition

The nineteenth century

1801 Ireland unites with Britain

In response to rebellions by the Irish, the British Prime Minister William Pitt persuaded the Irish Parliament to abolish itself and come under direct rule of the British Parliament.

Union Jack

Irish flag of St. Patrick

Scottish flag of St. Andrew

English flag of St. George

The Act of Union in 1801 united the two countries, which became known as the United Kingdom of Great Britain and Ireland. The Union Jack is made up from flags of England, Ireland and Scotland.

1805 The Battle of Trafalgar

After the French Revolution in 1789, France's leader, Napoleon Bonaparte carved out an empire on the continent of Europe. This led to a war between Britain and France. Napoleon planned to invade Britain, but in 1805 the French were defeated at sea at the Battle of Trafalgar by Admiral Nelson, who was killed in action. Napoleon was finally defeated in 1815 at the Battle of Waterloo.

1811 The Luddites

In the early years of the nineteenth century, there was a growing use of new machines in the textile industry. Many workers lost their jobs which led to riots and demonstrations. Rioters became known as the Luddites, named after a man called Ned Ludd, who was known for destroying machinery. *Unemployed workers*

1825 Stockton to Darlington railway

In 1825, Britain's first public railway opened between Stockton and Darlington. It was the first passenger-carrying railway in the world, though it mainly carried goods.

The Locomotion steam engine which ran between Stockton and Darlington.

1833 The Factory Act

The Factory Act of 1833 banned factory work for children under nine. Reformers continued to campaign to improve the terrible pay and conditions in Britain's factories and mines.

A child mineworker

1833 Slavery is banned

In 1833, Parliament passed William Wilberforce's bill banning British ships from taking part in slavery. This inhuman trade had been going on since the sixteenth century. Slaves were taken from Africa and shipped to the Americas, where they were sold to buy sugar and cotton for Europe.

The Wedgwood Medallion – a famous anti-slavery symbol

1834 The Tolpuddle Martyrs

In 1834, six men from Tolpuddle in Dorset were deported to Australia for trying to set up a local trade union. Although this in itself was not illegal, they were convicted because they had sworn an illegal oath of loyalty to each other. Their deportation caused a huge public outcry and two years later their sentence was withdrawn.

1838 The Chartists

In 1832, the Reform Act had given the vote to men of the middle classes, so that more men had a say in government. Demands continued, however, to extend the right to vote. A group called the Chartists was set up in 1838 to campaign for more reform, including votes for all men.

1839 The first Opium War

British traders supplied Chinese merchants with the drug opium, which was banned in China. The Chinese government was angry about this and two wars broke out, one from 1839-42 and the second from 1856-60. China was defeated in both and the British forced it to hand over territory, including Hong Kong, for trading purposes.

Chinese porcelain was sought after by European traders.

1851 The Great Exhibition

Queen Victoria came to the throne in 1837 and her reign was a time of wealth and success for Britain. Britain was known as "the workshop of the world". In 1851 a world trade exhibition was set up in London. Known as the Great Exhibition, a huge glass building, called the Crystal Palace, was built to house it.

The Crystal Palace. It later burned down in a fire.

1854 The Charge of the Light Brigade

In 1854, Britain fought the Crimean War in support of Turkey against Russia. Although victorious, the British were badly organized. At Balaclava, the Light Horse Brigade armed only with swords was ordered to charge at Russian cannons. Out of 673 men, 247 died. Soldiers also died of disease. Florence Nightingale, a nurse in the Crimea, helped to change the plight of soldiers by providing better food and health care.

Nurses in the Crimea

1857 The Indian Mutiny

By this time the British ruled India, but many Indians resented interference in their social and religious way of life. In 1857, Indian soldiers mutinied against their British officers. The rebellion spread and was not stopped until 1858.

Indian soldiers besiege the British residency at Lucknow.

1863 The London Underground

In 1863, the first underground railway in the world opened in London. It ran between Paddington and the City. It was known as the Metropolitan Railway.

The London Underground sign

1871 Stanley meets Dr. Livingstone

Stanley meets Livingstone.

From the late 1850s, a Scottish doctor and missionary named David Livingstone was exploring Africa. He spent many years there and had a personal mission to fight the slave trade. In Europe he was given up for lost, but in 1871 H. M. Stanley succeeded in finding him. He greeted him with the famous words "Dr. Livingstone, I presume". From the 1870s, European countries were increasingly anxious to gain colonies in Africa, due to its abundance of natural resources. This is sometimes called the "scramble for Africa".

1876 Victoria becomes Empress of India

In 1876, Queen Victoria took the title "Empress of India", to set up a special relationship between the monarchy and India. It succeeded in winning the queen loyalty in India.

After her husband Albert died in 1861, Victoria always wore black.

1899 The Boer War

In 1899 a war broke out in southern Africa between the British and the Boers – descendents of Dutch settlers. Britain had expanded into Boer territory, which the Boers resented. The war ended in 1901 and a new state was created, with the aim of sharing power between the British and the Boers. This new country was called the Union of South Africa.

The Queen's South Africa medal, awarded to British soldiers who fought in the Boer War

The twentieth century

A union banner

1906 The Labour Party

In 1900, trade unions and socialist groups came together to form one of the first political parties for the working class. Called the Labour Representation Committee, it was renamed the Labour Party in 1906.

1912 The Titanic goes down

In 1912, a great disaster happened at sea which shocked the world. The *Titanic*, a new liner on her maiden voyage, set off to New York from Britain. The ship had been declared unsinkable, but in the freezing waters of the North Atlantic, the ship struck an iceberg and sank within hours. Only 711 people survived out of 2,224. The disaster led to more concern about safety at sea, and especially the use of radio communication.

1914 World War One

In 1914, World War One broke out, as Britain, France and Russia fought against Austria and Germany. In 1916, one of the bloodiest battles in history took place near the River Somme in France. Men fought in terrible conditions across fields of mud and barbed wire. One and a quarter million troops were killed in the battle which raged for six months. Britain and its allies finally won the war in 1918, but at great loss of life to all sides.

Soldiers lived, fought and died in muddy trenches.

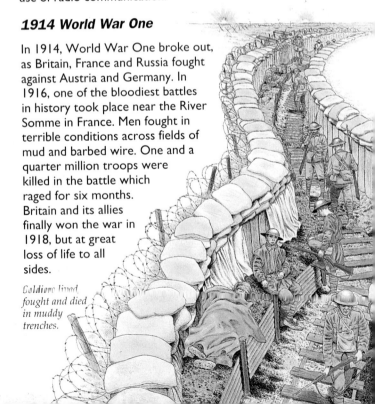

The flag of
Northern Ireland

NORTHERN
IRELAND

IRISH
FREE STATE
(1921)

The flag of Eire,
or the Republic
of Ireland

1916 The Easter Rising

In 1914, plans were laid to allow Ireland to govern itself (called "home rule"). Tension continued between the Catholic majority in the south who wanted home rule and the Protestants in the north who didn't. In Dublin in 1916, rebels tried to declare an Irish republic. Dublin was soon ablaze as British soldiers stopped the rebellion, which became known as the Easter Rising. Fifteen rebel leaders were executed.

In 1921, the British and Irish governments agreed that southern Ireland should become the Irish Free State (which was later renamed Eire). Six provinces in northern Ireland remained part of the United Kingdom.

1919 Votes for women

Before World War One, women were not allowed to vote. Some women, called Suffragettes, campaigned for this right. When war broke out, many women took on jobs traditionally done by men, while the men were away fighting. This proved to the men in power that women were capable of an active role in society. In 1919 women over the age of 30 were given the right to vote.

A suffragette protest

1936 The Jarrow March

In the 1930s there was a world economic crisis, called the Great Depression. Many people lost jobs and were desperately poor. In 1936, a group of men from a shipbuilding town called Jarrow in the northeast of England, went on a 483km (300 mile) march to London to draw attention to their plight.

Men on the Jarrow March

1936 Edward VIII abdicates

In January 1936, Edward VIII came to the throne. He was in love with an American named Wallis Simpson. Because she had been divorced, she was not acceptable to Britain or the Empire as queen. In December the King decided to abdicate (give up his throne). His decision shocked the world.

Edward and Wallis

1939 World War Two

In the late 1930s, the German leader Adolf Hitler built up the German army and occupied territory in Europe, which was against the treaties made after World War One. Britian and France hoped to prevent war by appeasement – giving in to Hitler's demands. This policy of appeasement, however, didn't work. In September 1939 Germany invaded Poland, so France and Britain declared war. In 1940, German forces swept across Belgium, the Netherlands and France, which all fell under German control.

A flag bearer from Hitler's Nazi Party

1940 The Battle of Britain

In 1940, the Germans launched a series of air attacks against Britain in the hope of knocking out its air force and clearing the way for an invasion. For four months a battle was fought in the skies above southern Britain, but Hitler failed to win supremacy. This fight is called the Battle of Britain.

British Spitfire

German Messerschmidt

28

1940 The Blitz

After the German air force failed to win the Battle of Britain, Hitler changed his tactics. His bombers now undertook night missions against big British cities. This attack lasted from September 1940 to May 1941. It became known as the Blitz.

Sheltering from bombs underground.

1944 D-Day

Winston Churchill, Prime Minister during World War Two

In 1941, Japan entered the war on Germany's side and the USA became Britain's ally. On June 6, 1944, British, Canadian and American forces took part in the invasion of Normandy, France. The first day of the invasion was code-named D-Day. It took a month of fighting to break away from the coast, but they were at last able to continue the advance towards Germany. Facing defeat, Hitler committed suicide and Germany surrendered in May 1945.

1946 The Welfare State

In 1945, the Labour Party came to power with the task of rebuilding the economy and improving social conditions. The government set up the Welfare State in 1946. This was a system of social services, such as old-age pensions and unemployment benefit, paid for by taxes. In 1948, the National Health Service followed, providing free health care for all.

1947 Independent India

Weakened by war, European nations were no longer able to hold on to their colonies abroad. The colonies increased their demands for independence and many achieved their wish to be free. In 1947, India became the first to gain independence after a campaign by the National Congress Party.

Mahatma Gandhi – leader of the Indian National Congress Party.

1949 *The Iron Curtain divides Europe*

The US flag

After the war, relations became tense between the democratic USA and Western Europe on one side, and the Communist Soviet Union and Eastern Europe on the other.

The Soviet flag

In 1949, Britain joined the North Atlantic Treaty Organization (NATO), set up by the Western powers for mutual protection. In response, the eastern nations formed the Warsaw Pact. This mistrust, known as the Cold War, lasted until the late 1980s. The division in Europe became known as the Iron Curtain.

1973 *Britain joins the EEC*

In 1973, Britain joined the European Economic Community (EEC), also called the Common Market. This organization promoted and regulated trade

Flags of the first 12 EEC member nations

between its members. It was originally set up in 1957, but Britain delayed joining because it was worried that the EEC rules would affect its trade links with its former colonies overseas. The EEC is now called the EC (European Community).

1976 *Concorde*

In 1976, the first supersonic (faster than the speed of sound) passenger jet went into service. Called *Concorde*, the jet was a joint development by Britain and France.

Concorde flies across the Atlantic Ocean in just three hours and forty minutes. It normally takes eight hours.

1982 The Falklands Crisis

In 1979, Margaret Thatcher became Prime Minister – the first woman to hold the position. In 1982, she faced one of the biggest crises of her premiership, when Argentinian forces invaded the Falkland Islands, one of Britain's few remaining colonies. Britain waged ten weeks of undeclared war against Argentina in the South Atlantic. Troops and warships were sent to regain the islands and Argentina surrendered.

1992 The Maastricht Treaty

On February 7, 1992, representatives of the twelve EC members met in the small Dutch town of Maastricht to sign two treaties. The treaties set down broad outlines for a closer European union. In the future, they agreed, Europeans would share common citizenship, economic and defensive policies. Britain ratified (gave formal approval to) the Maastricht Treaty in August 1993.

1993 The Downing Street Declaration

In 1968, a new wave of violence had begun in Northern Ireland as Catholic and Protestant terrorists fought each other. British troops were sent to help combat unrest, but bombings and shootings continued.

In December 1993, the British Prime Minister John Major and the Irish Prime Minister Albert Reynolds issued the Downing Street Declaration – a plan for peace talks. It was the first real step in the direction of future peace.

1996 Ceasefire broken

British soldier in Northern Ireland

A ceasefire, negotiated by Britain and Ireland, was followed by plans for peace talks and terrorist disarmament. But in 1996, the ceasefire was broken by an IRA (Irish Republican Army) bomb in London's dockland. Plans for talks still went ahead.

Index

Acknowledgements

This book is illustrated by: Stephen Conlin, Peter Dennis, Richard
Draper, Nicholas Hewetson, Ian Jackson, Colin King, Ross Watton and
Gerald Wood.

The publishers would like to thank the following for permission to
reproduce their photographs: p23 Waterford Wedgwood; p28, p31
Hulton Deutsch.